This book belongs to:

_____

_____

Contents

First published 2006 by Brown Watson
The Old Mill, 76 Fleckney Road,
Kibworth Beauchamp, Leic LE8 0HG

ISBN: 0-7097-1743-1

EARLY READERS

3 Happytime Stories

Stories by Gill Davies

Illustrations by:
Gill Guile, Stephen Holmes,
Jane Swift and Lawrie Taylor

Brown Watson

ENGLAND

MAX IS SAD

Max Motorbike can race.
He races as fast as a train. As
he races he shouts, "Watch me
go! The best in the show!"

Then one day, Max stops.
His wheels will not work
any more.

"You are old now," says his
driver. "You are too old to race.
You are no use to me
any more."

He takes Max to a man who collects old cars and bikes.

Max has to stay still all day. People look at him and say, "What an old motorbike."

Max is sad. He is so sad that he sobs. Big tears run down his sad, red face.

Then one day some boys and girls come into the room.

"What a super motorbike," the boy says. "Can we take him to our park? We need a new ride."

Their father buys Max. Then he puts him on the roundabout in the park.

Now at last Max can race again.

"I love it here," he says. "I can race fast every day. Watch me go! The best in the show! Wheee!"

KEY WORDS

boys	more
buy	park
cars	room
race	show
every	their
fast	train
father	use
girls	work

WHAT CAN YOU SEE HERE?

handlebars

motorbike

park

man

roundabout

POLLY PUP'S CLEVER TRICK

"Who likes dirt? I do," says Polly Pup. "I like dirt. I like rolling in it. I like jumping in it. I like getting it all over me."

Polly runs away to paddle in the puddles and roll in even more mud.

"Come back," calls Mrs Green. "Come back," calls Woof the dog.

"What a mess," says Mrs Green.

Woof the Dog goes to
find Polly.

"Polly! Come here!" calls
Woof. "It is time to have
a bath."

Polly runs into the barn.
"What a mess you are,"
says Horse. You need a bath."

Polly runs into the garden.
"What a mess you are," says
Mouse. You need a bath."

"No I don't,"
barks Polly. She
runs into the house.

Polly runs into the bathroom.

"No-one will find me now," says Polly. "No-one will find me here in the bathroom. They think I am running away from the bath."

Clever Polly is right. No-one looks for her there. So she settles down for a nice sleep on the muddy, muddy mat and dreams of making even more mess tomorrow.

KEY WORDS

away	house
back	like
calls	me
find	Mrs
garden	nice
goes	sleep
green	there
here	who

WHAT CAN YOU SEE HERE?

mud

barn

Polly Pup

bath

hedge

LET'S PRETEND

The sun is shining. It is a hot, hot day. It is the sort of day to go to the sea and paddle.

So Rag Doll says to all the toys, "I shall make our very own seaside right here."

Pig helps her to find the bag of sand and all the toy fish on strings.

Soon lots of happy little fish bob up and down.

"This is a very nice seaside," they say, as Rag Doll finds a box of treasure in the toy box.

"Let's play at being pirates, too," she says. "We can hide our treasure in the sand."

At last everything is ready.

"Come and play!" calls Rag Doll. "We have our very own seaside here now. We have our very own pirate's treasure too - and lots and lots of sand."

All the toys run over to play.

"Look at all those funny fish," says Duck.

"This is the best toy seaside ever!" says Rabbit.
"Three cheers for Rag Doll."

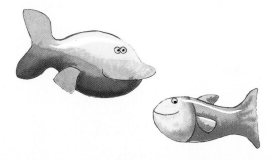

KEY WORDS

at	lots
box	own
doll	rabbit
everything	ready
her	sea
hot	so
last	soon
let's	sun

WHAT CAN YOU SEE HERE?

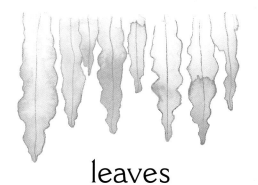

leaves

Rag Doll

treasure

fish